NOVELIZATION

Printed in the United States of America
First Paperback Edition, September 2021
1 3 5 7 9 10 8 6 4 2
FAC-025438-21204

Library of Congress Control Number: 2020951841
ISBN 978-1-368-07281-6

For more Disney Press fun, visit www.disneybooks.com
Visit DisneyChannel.com and DisneyPlus.com

SUSTAINABLE
FORESTRY
INITIATIVE
Certified Chain of Custody
Promoting Sustainable Forestry
www.sfiprogram.org
SFI-01054
The SFI label applies to the text stock

NOVELIZATION

Adapted by Carin Davis

Based on the screenplay by Doan La

𝕯𝖎𝖘𝖓𝖊𝖞 PRESS
Los Angeles • New York

CHAPTER 1

Christmastime in Chicago was nothing short of magical. The holiday spirit rushed through the Windy City like a gust off the lakefront. The Lincoln Park Zoo lights twinkled beneath the flurrying snow, the slick ice-skating ribbon twisted through Maggie Daley Park, and the holiday CTA train transformed commuting on the L into a sleigh-like experience. For twelve-year-old Rowena "Ro" Clybourne, it was the most wonderful, most dazzling, most spectacular time of the year.

Or at least it used to be.

On Christmas Eve, Ro burrowed in a nest of quilts on her twin bed while commenting on viral holiday videos on a laptop "borrowed" from her older sister, Gabriela. She watched for the third time the one with the dog dressed as Rudolph. . . . Yup, still hilarious. She was about to hit play a fourth time when her mom, Carolina, knocked. Ro scrambled, slamming the computer shut and shoving it beneath her bed. No point in getting placed on the naughty list just hours before Santa's arrival.

Carolina peeked around the door. "Are you still up? Everyone's coming early tomorrow."

"Relax, Mom. Getting up early on Christmas is what I do best," bragged Ro. She and Santa were totally in sync on that one.

Carolina glanced around Ro's room. Muddy sneakers lay abandoned on the floor, clothes were piled high on the desk chair, and a scuffed-up ball had rolled under the dresser. "Ay, ay, yi, what a mess! I thought we agreed you'd clean up."

"I wanted to, but I was so excited for Christmas."

Her mom bent down and picked up a nutcracker soldier from the floor. The stiff wooden figure had been hiding beneath a tie-dyed T-shirt and a discarded jersey. "I didn't know you still had this," Carolina said, smiling and standing the soldier at attention atop Ro's dresser.

"I love that thing. It reminds me of the Christmas when we all went to see *The Nutcracker*," Ro said.

"I'm surprised you remember. You were so young."

"Well, I slept through half of it. But the other half really landed. It almost made my list. Look. . . ."

Ro reached for a piece of crumpled paper on top of her quilt. On it was a handwritten list, dutifully color-coded and decorated with holiday doodles.

Carolina sat on the edge of her daughter's bed, leaned in, and read the list aloud.

ROWENA'S TOP 5 CHRISTMAS MEMORIES

Number 5: The *Christmas Around the World* exhibit at the museum

"Aww, that's where we took that picture of you and Gabriela under the big tree," Carolina said.

Number 4: The Pier

Ro jumped in. "Remember? We got to see all the holiday performers! I got to ride on the Ferris wheel! That was a classic!" She chuckled.

Number 3: The Santas vs. Elves hockey match

"Which Dad and I will definitely want to watch tomorrow." Ro drew a thick, confident check mark with her feather-topped pen. Every Christmas Day, she and her dad took their heaping plates of food into the study, where they hunkered down together to watch the annual grudge match on ice. Ro was sure this would be the year their beloved Santas outscored those pesky Elves.

Number 2: That big platform thingy

Carolina's blank look revealed she had no idea what her daughter was talking about.

"That giant platform thingy that opens out so you feel like you're flying over the city?" explained Ro.

"Right. At the top of the Hancock building. But you were too scared to even step on it."

"But I watched Gabby do it. From only a few feet away. The look on her face was priceless." Ro grinned ear to ear at the thought of her sister's panic. "And my number one favorite Christmas memory . . ."

Number 1: Winterfest!

"Obvi . . ."

"Obvi . . ." Carolina concurred.

"Can we go back to Winterfest tomorrow, Mom? Please?"

"Honey, we might have to switch things up a little bit this year," Carolina said. "It's our first Christmas with some new faces."

Ro grimaced. "You mean Diane. And Louie." Saying the names aloud left a sour taste on her tongue.

"Honey, I know these memories mean a lot to you. But, hey, we can make new memories. Christmas isn't only about tradition. It's about us all being together, despite the changes."

Ro had met her dad's girlfriend, Diane, and her six-year-old son, Louie, just once before, when he brought them over for Thanksgiving. Diane ran an organic bakery. She showed up on Turkey Day carrying quinoa muffins with cashew-milk frosting, claiming Ro wouldn't be able to tell the difference. . . . She could. It was bad enough that her parents had split without her dad bringing a stranger and her kid to their holiday dinner. And now it was happening again. On Christmas.

"But I don't want anything to change," Ro told her mom.

"I know you don't, honey, but sometimes change is for the best, like cleaning your room every once in a while!" Carolina smothered her daughter with playful pinches and tickles. Ro made as if to swat her mom away, but it was clear she loved the affection.

"All right, lights out, you," sang Carolina. "Or someone's not getting a visit from Santa." She tucked her daughter in and turned out the light on the bed stand.

"Buenos noches, mijita."

"Buenos noches, Mama."

CHAPTER 2

Ro awoke with a start, her penguin-shaped alarm clock blaring a jolly rendition of "Jingle Bells" at full volume. Right. In. Her. Ear.

"Jingle bells! Jingle bells! Jingle all the way! Oh, what fun . . ."

As the song faded, an overly chipper DJ chimed, "Good morning, Chicago. It's the day you've all been waiting for! It's—"

"Christmas!" cheered another DJ in unison.

Ro slowly sat up in her tangle of blankets. The hairs on her neck prickled as a ghostly figure rose from the side of her bed.

"Boo," said the sheet-covered ghost.

Ro jumped up from her bed, then tripped over her skateboard and crashed into the dresser, where the proud nutcracker stood. The wooden soldier wobbled, then toppled, then smashed to pieces as he hit the deck. The skateboard flew backward and slammed into Ro's nightstand, spilling a half-drunk glass of orange juice all over Gabby's laptop. Gabby was gonna be mad.

The ghost started giggling at the chaos. Ro knew that laugh. The ghost ripped off the white sheet, revealing a familiar snickering little boy. "Louie!" she shouted. "Oh, you're gonna get it." Louie took off, and Ro bolted from her room and down the stairs, hot on his tail, until the kid leapt from the bottom stair, Superman-style, into the outstretched arms of Ro's dad, Mike.

"Gotcha, you little devil!" said Mike, wrapping the squirming boy in his arms. "Were you having fun upstairs?" Ro's dad was a warm, easygoing guy. His good nature radiated from beneath his rugged looks, and his eyes twinkled when he spotted his daughter.

"Yeah, I was having lots of fun with Ro," he said.

"Hey, sprout," whooped Mike. "Merry Christmas!"

"Merry Christmas, Dad," Ro said, smiling. Father and daughter broke out in a long-practiced elaborate handshake.

"Dad, why didn't you wake me like you always do?" Ro asked above the hand-clapping and palm-slapping.

"I wanted to, but Louie asked to do the honors. Looks like he got the job done."

"She's totally up," Louie said with a snicker.

"Yeah, she is," Mike said, carrying Louie toward the kitchen. "Ro, come say hi to Diane."

Ro could have stayed in the foyer talking with her father for hours; there was loads to fill him in on: her math grade, batting practice, her thoughts on the Bears' playoff chances. But instead, she followed her dad and Louie into the kitchen.

"Guess who decided to join us," announced Mike.

"Morning, sleepy head," her mom said. She was already busy preparing for the big holiday meal.

Gabby and Diane were trying to do some dance move that was on Gabby's phone screen. *Ugh.* Diane was wearing a flowing dress, with perfect hair that Ro was sure had taken her an hour to get just right. She wasn't buying that the natural-foods baker was naturally always this put-together.

"Rowena! Merry Christmas!" said Diane, clapping with a bit too much effort and enthusiasm. "Your dad told me that you made the softball team. What position do you play?"

"Goalie."

"Roooooo," warned Mike, the drawn-out pronunciation of her name a thinly veiled code for "knock it off."

"Okay, shortstop," admitted Ro, unfolding her list from her pocket. "Hey, Dad, I made a list of all my favorite Christmas memories for us to do again. Which do you want to do first?"

Mike glanced at the long, color-coded list, then at Diane and Louie. "Gee, I dunno, sprout. I think your mom's planning a nice day for everyone. We might have to play it by ear."

"But we can at least watch the Santas versus Elves match, can't we? This has gotta be the Santas' year," declared Ro.

Mike smiled at his girl, his eyes crinkling. "I hope so,

after the last two beatdowns. Although, I'm hearing the Santas' center is out with spasms."

"Again?" groaned Ro. "That guy should really stretch. Do you think we can still—"

"What's a center?" interrupted Louie. Mike turned his attention to the little boy.

"A position in hockey. Usually the middle player on the forward line."

Ro continued. "Do you think we can—"

"What are spasms?" cut in Louie.

"Something you won't have to worry about for a long time," Mike said, marveling at the kid's curiosity. Then he turned back to Ro. "Sorry, sweetheart, what were you asking me?"

"Do you think the Santas can still—"

"Shoelaces!" demanded Louie, presenting his foot to Mike. While her dad dutifully tied the laces, Ro huffed and went to the Advent calendar on the counter to seek solace in what lay inside the last wooden drawer. She opened it carefully. Empty.

"Who took the last chocolate?" Ro scanned the room, her eyes piercing the faces of her sister, her mom, her dad . . . and finally resting on Diane, who froze mid-chew, taste buds guilty with chocolate.

"Maybe Santa was hungry last night," said Mike, attempting to melt the icy tension between his daughter and his girlfriend.

"Don't give me that, Dad. I'm not a little baby like Louie," said Ro.

"Watch it, Ro," warned Carolina.

"But, Mom, we trade off every year who gets the last chocolate. This was supposed to be my year."

Diane sighed sheepishly. "It was me. I'm sorry, Rowena. I didn't know about your tradition."

Before Ro could lament the injustice of her Advent chocolate, Louie leapt in and stole the moment. "Look what I can do!" he said, flailing his arms and legs in what Ro could only guess were supposed to be tap dance moves.

"Aww, Louie, that's wonderful," gushed Carolina.

Diane nodded in agreement. "He's only had one class."

Mike took Diane's hand; they marveled as Louie shuffled off to Buffalo. Ro gaped. Was no one else seeing what she was seeing? Louie was no Gene Kelly. His feet thrashed around without style or skill.

Gabby noted her little sister's shock. "Hope you asked Santa for a blankie. 'Cause it's gonna be cold outta that spotlight," she teased.

CHAPTER
3

Christmas **morning** was not unfolding as Ro had planned. But she felt better the minute her abuela Sofia and abuelo Hector arrived. Not just because they carried armloads of gifts, but because Ro's grandparents put the *feliz* in *Feliz Navidad*. The house felt warmer with them in it. Abuelo was an ebullient retired physician with a huge heart; he always made Ro laugh. Abuela was a former teacher whose smile radiated kindness. The boisterous couple greeted everyone in Spanish and dusted the snow from their hats.

"You two are looking lively, indeed. How was midnight mass?" asked Mike, kissing Sofia on the cheek.

"Absolutely transporting," she said. Ro's abuela found the late-night service invigorating and attended every year. Some things never changed, but alas, some—like Ro's parents' marriage—did, and the family was adjusting to the shifts. Abuela Sofia glanced at Mike's girlfriend, whom she had met at Thanksgiving, and smiled warmly, trying to make the moment less awkward. "Oh, Diane, it's so good to see you."

"It's good to see you, Sofia. And you, too, Hector." Diane's voice sounded formal and stiff.

"Diane, por favor, I already told you, all my friends call me Doc!" bellowed Hector.

"Well, Merry Christmas, Doc," she said.

Sofia turned her attention to her granddaughter. She spun Ro to get a good look at her, then cupped her face in her hands and peppered her forehead and cheeks with red-lipstick kisses. "Oh, my little Rowena! Did you like the sweater? I made it myself."

"We haven't opened presents yet, Mom," Carolina said, laughing.

"But thanks for the spoiler," joked Ro.

"All right, you'll smother the poor girl," said Hector, smiling at his wife. "Ro, are we having a nice Christmas?"

Ro wasn't sure how to answer that. She'd been scared

awake by Louie and cheated out of the last Advent chocolate. So yeah . . . so far, not so stellar. But now that her grandparents were in the house, it was beginning to feel a lot like Christmas. And once her uncles made their grand entrance, everything would be—

Ro's thoughts were interrupted by the loud rumblings of Abuela Sofia's tummy.

Abuelo heard them, too. "Cómo está, mi amor? It's my fault. I should never have dragged you to that greasy spoon diner." He leaned in to hug his wife and accidentally dropped his keys behind her.

Ro crouched to pick them up, then heard the warning grumble. "Oh, no," she said, but it was too late. Abuela Sofia released a rippling fart. "Ew! Sausage and eggs!" Ro said, dry heaving. Louie and Gabby laughed from their nearby seats.

Ro was still recovering from the smell when her uncle Gerry and his husband, Bruce, arrived at the front door. Uncle Gerry had met his art-dealer husband, Bruce, years before in the produce section of the grocery store.

"Merry Christmas," yelped Ro and Carolina. Her uncles simultaneously shushed them, then returned to quietly cooing over a swaddled fuzz ball in Gerry's arms.

"You got a dog?" shouted Ro at a decibel that matched her unbridled excitement. The startled puppy awoke.

"Perfect. She's awake again," sighed Gerry.

"We adopted Olive from the shelter," Bruce explained. "She kept us up all night barking."

"Want to hold her?" Uncle Gerry asked, handing the dog to Ro as he and Bruce entered the house. "Here she is." Before Ro could win the pup's affection, Diane came to greet the fluffy new family member.

"Who do we have here?" she cooed, taking the dog into her arms. "It's a good thing you're not a cat, 'cause cats make me so sneezy! Hey, I know a little boy who'd love to meet you!"

Everyone followed Diane and Olive back into the house, leaving Ro standing by herself near the front door.

"Uncle Gerry?" she said, feeling like everyone had forgotten all about her.

Ro thought her Christmas couldn't get much worse. She was wrong.

CHAPTER
4

Ro sat beneath the ornament-filled Christmas tree, surrounded by an explosion of boxes, gift bags, and baskets. The present in her hands was from her mom.

"It's a scrapbook. And paper," said Carolina.

Ro stared at the craft project before her. "But, Mom, you always get me clothes."

"Which you never like," her mom noted. "You always complain."

"At first," said Ro. "But then you make me try them on and I low-key love them. That's like our thing, Mom! Why are you messing with the program?"

"I'll still buy you clothes," Carolina said. "I just thought you might like something new."

"This is definitely new, all right."

"I made cookies," Diane announced as she whisked into the room carrying a big platter. Ro grabbed a cookie, hoping to seek solace in chocolate chips. She inspected the sweet. It smelled suspicious. "Is there kale in this?"

"There is indeed!" Diane said, smiling. "You've got a great nose! These are my best sellers."

Ro tossed the cookie back onto the plate, then wadded up a ball of wrapping paper and tossed it to the floor.

Carolina grabbed the used wrapping paper and stuffed it into a garbage bag. "Honey, pick up after yourself. Someone's gonna break their neck."

"But this is what we do every year, Mom. Gabby and I make a mess so you can get mad and clean up."

"Ro, that is not funny. And if you're trying to make me mad, it's working," scolded Carolina.

Ro reached for another box and tore into the paper, spreading the shreds everywhere. Inside the box was a theatrical makeup kit. *Huh?*

Diane, eager to find a bonding point with her boyfriend's daughter, could barely contain her excitement. "Do you like it? Your dad told me you were in the school play."

"In third grade." Ro stared at the blue eye shadow palette, the three shades of rouge, and the potpourri of lip gloss colors. "My favorite part was definitely the makeup." Her tone was nothing short of sarcastic.

"No way," exclaimed Louie, excited by a new archery toy he had just unwrapped. He fired an arrow in Ro's direction. She crumpled up another wrapping paper ball and chucked it toward the little boy.

"Honey, come on! You're killing me," said Carolina, picking up after her daughter.

Ro ignored her mom, choosing instead to cheer herself up by unwrapping another gift.

"This one is from your uncles," said Uncle Bruce. Beneath the layers of wrapping paper and tissue sat a crisp white martial arts robe.

"This, Ro, is what we call a judogi. It's what all true judokas wear." Finally—a cool gift.

"I got one, too!" yelled Louie from across the room. "Twinsies! Hiyah!" He tried his best judo kick, but his judo was as bad as his tap-dancing.

Everyone turned their attention to Louie, and Ro no longer felt like her gift was special.

"Louie, that is really cute," Carolina declared.

Ro grabbed another gift from the bottom of the stack. It was from her dad. And Diane. Her dad knew her better than anyone. This was sure to be the gift of the day.

"All right, sprout," gushed Mike, "you're gonna like this one. I noticed yours was getting old, so we got you—"

In her hands, Ro held a flat golden rectangle with a gray screen. "A tablet! With knobs?" Ro searched for a button to turn it on. Unable to find one, she wondered if this model had fingerprint security or facial recognition.

"That's a classic!" exclaimed her abuelo. "Mija, you turn those knobs to draw, then shake it up and qué milagro! Like it never happened."

Mike winced. "I think there's been a mix-up."

On the other side of the room, Louie shrieked with glee, barely able to control his delirium. On his tiny hand he wore a brand-new adult-sized brown leather softball glove.

"Awesome! I love it so much! Thank you! Can we play catch now? Can we?" begged Louie, grabbing Mike's hand to pull him outside to play.

Ro frowned as Louie raised the prized softball glove high in the air, as if he'd just won the World Series of presents—which he had.

Still holding Louie's hand, Mike turned his head to look at his daughter, the shortstop. "I'm sorry, sprout. We'll figure it out. Hey, why don't you grab your glove and meet us outside?"

"That was my glove," Ro said to no one in particular.

Abuela Sofia took in the scene and then took charge. Christmas gifts were supposed to bring joy, cheer, and love, and she had just the gift to accomplish all three. She carefully unwrapped tissue paper from a vibrant vintage serving bowl. Its artistry was stunning; its importance clear. "Carolina, your father and I want to give you something very special. This was given to us, and it has been in our family for generations. It was passed down to me from my bisabuela Lucia from Puerto Rico, who had it passed from her tatarabuela Maribel. I still remember her serving arroz con gandules in this."

"Gracias, Mama," Carolina said, clearly touched by the gift. "I love it. I love it."

Gabby reached into a pile of presents to retrieve her phone to take a picture. She pulled up Olive's slimy chew toy instead. "Ew! Dog slobber!" she yelped, flinging the drool-soaked ball onto Ro's lap, who tossed it toward Abuelo, causing him to upend the antique.

"Noooooooooooooooo," cried Abuela. Her bisabuela's pottery careered through the air, spinning as it went, before plummeting toward the hardwood floor. Using his judo reflexes, Uncle Bruce leapt up and caught the ceramic in his hand mere inches from its demise. Relief spread across everyone's face.

"And to think all the kids used to call me butterfingers. Ha!" said Bruce. The family broke out in joyous applause, recognizing a Christmas miracle when they saw one. But just as Bruce was about to take a bow, he slipped on a piece of Ro's discarded wrapping paper, lost his balance, and fell to the ground. The bowl followed with an ugly crunch. The generations-old serving bowl shattered into jagged pieces beside him.

"I'm okay," a disappointed Bruce announced.

All eyes turned from the guilty piece of wrapping paper to Ro.

"Okay, well that just happened. Um, so, guess I'll go look for my glove," she said, turning away from her family's glares.

Ro retreated up the stairs in search of her mitt. Mike was the one who'd first taught Ro how to play softball. They'd spent hours on the front lawn after dinner perfecting her throw. Before the divorce, he used to attend all her games. Ro scanned her messy room. The glove had to be there somewhere—under the bed or beneath the laundry. She opened her closet to find Olive inside, chewing on her glove. "Well, at least you didn't pee on it," said Ro before hearing a slow tinkling sound. "Aaaand you just peed on it. Cool."

Ro picked up the soiled glove with two fingers. Through her bedroom window, she saw her dad on the front lawn teaching Louie how to throw, just as he'd done with her. Mike saw Ro in the window and motioned for her to come down.

Louie was wearing Ro's new glove on his hand. Diane cheered them on, clapping her mittened hands together. Ro watched the threesome for another minute, then walked to her garbage can and tossed her glove in the trash.

CHAPTER 5

This year Christmas dinner was being served buffet style. Ro reluctantly joined everyone else as they crammed together in the family room, balancing plates piled high with food on their knees. Her abuelos held court in the two comfiest chairs. Her uncles claimed one end of the couch, with Olive curled up between them, while Carolina sat on the other end. Ro was relegated to a seat on the floor next to Gabby and Louie, while her dad and Diane sat on chairs from the dining room. Ro'd been hoping Mike would sit with them.

"I'm done eating," Ro announced mid-bite. "Can Dad and I go watch the rest of the match?"

"Sprout, I just sat down," Mike said. "And last I

checked, it pains me to say, the Elves are crushing my Santas."

Carolina jumped in. "Honey, you can go after everyone's had dinner and dessert. I made gingerbread cake!"

"Did somebody say 'gingerbread'?" Uncle Gerry stood.

Carolina shook her finger. "Espérate un momentito, Hermano, because last year you didn't save any for the kids, so I'm instituting a one slice rule para ti."

Gerry switched into lawyer mode, pleading his case. "That is a baseless accusation! I could sue you for defamation! Or you can cough up the gingerbread."

"Or, I know, we should make him perform for his cake," offered Bruce. He knew something about his partner that the family didn't. "Gerry's been taking a stand-up class."

"Bruce! You said you wouldn't tell!"

"Mom," pleaded Ro over the ruckus. "The match is almost over."

Carolina threw up her hands. "Fine. You can go watch. But first finish your dinner."

Ro scooped the last couple of bites of mashed potatoes into her mouth in record time. She and her dad could still make it for the third period, just in time to watch the Santas launch a comeback.

"Stand-up comedy?" asked Mike, making no move to leave. "Gerry, that's awesome."

Bruce bragged on his partner's behalf. "He's still a tad shy. Hey, why don't you do that bit you're working on?"

"Bruce, I'm still working on it," said Gerry.

But the whole family chanted, "Do it! Do it!" until Gerry surrendered. "Okay, just be kind because it's still a work in progress. Okay, here goes nothing. . . ."

Ro pushed her plate aside and stood up. "All done! Come on, Dad! Let's go!"

"Rowena, sit," Carolina demanded.

Ro rolled her eyes and sat back down. She could tell from her mother's tone that she was not going anywhere until after Uncle Gerry's comedy routine.

Uncle Gerry held a spoon to his mouth like a microphone and launched into his bit. "Okay, so I'm a lawyer, right, as you already know. And the hardest part of being a lawyer is turning off work mode when you get home."

Ro slapped her knees. "Ha! Hilarious, Uncle Gerry! Wonderful show. Well, we're off to watch some hockey," she said, standing up.

"Ro, he didn't get to the punch line," said Carolina. "Sit down." Everyone returned their attention to Gerry, now sweaty and flustered.

"Doing great, Ger," Bruce said encouragingly. "Work mode?"

Gerry cleared his throat and restarted his routine. "Right. The hardest part of being a lawyer is turning off work mode when you get home."

Ro tapped her foot. The third period had definitely started without her and her dad. "You already said that," she urged.

"Will you let your uncle tell his joke?" said Carolina.

"I'm just trying to help," said Ro. Wasn't her interruption technically an act of kindness, since her uncle wasn't funny?

But Gerry had had enough. "You know what? I just realized I don't even like gingerbread. I move to strike this discussion."

"Oh, come on, Gerry. Continue," said Carolina.

"It's okay, really," he said.

But the family still chanted, "Ger-ry! Ger-ry! Ger-ry!"

"I said no! I don't even want cake. Just leave me alone." Gerry stormed from the room. Bruce and Olive scurried after him.

Abuelo Hector and Abuela Sofia went into the dining room for seconds. Suddenly the tablecloth—and the food—started moving, and then everything crashed to the floor. The family rushed in to find Olive had tugged the tablecloth down and was nibbling on the turkey.

"My dinner!" exclaimed Carolina. Meanwhile, Gabby couldn't resist snapping a shot of the disaster with her phone.

"Well, clearly dinner's officially over!" Ro said, trying not to laugh. "Does anybody want to watch the match? Anybody?"

No one said a word.

Then Diane chimed in, "I will."

"Anyone else?" Ro asked, not exactly thrilled by Diane's offer.

★ ★ ★

While the family cleaned up Olive's mess, Ro finally got to indulge in the end of the hockey game. "Five minutes left in the match," said announcer Israel Idonije.

"The Santas are nearly out of time. Where is Rudolph when you need him?" proclaimed the other announcer, Hosea Sanders.

"Come on, Santas. D up!" Ro cheered. "Woo! Let's go!"

The Elves took the puck down the ice, barreling down on the Santas' defense . . . when the TV cut out mid-play.

"What? Come on!" cried Ro, staring at the blank screen. "Where is the remote?" Seconds later, the TV magically turned back on.

Ro returned to the on-screen action and the commentary. "Can you believe what is happening on the ice? The Elves are running away with this. It's gonna be awkward in Santa's Village to—" The TV cut out again. Ro jumped up, searching for the remote. She couldn't miss the end of the game. She was digging through piles of pillows when the TV came back to life inexplicably.

Ro sat back down; the TV shut off again. This time, she heard a giggle from the far corner of the room. She knew that giggle: it was Louie's.

"Gimme the remote, Louie," she yelped, spying the boy hiding behind a snowman decoration.

"Why?" he teased.

"So I can beat you with it," said Ro.

"Then no," declared Louie.

"I'm gonna count to three. One . . ."

"Catch!" shouted Louie, throwing just like Mike had taught him. The remote smashed into Ro's leg.

She charged at Louie, careful not to trip over the Christmas train. However, she got tangled in a string of lights, which set off a chain reaction of destruction. The decorations on the mantel tumbled to the floor. The family hurried in at the noise.

"Ro! What is going on?" Carolina chided.

"He started it," explained Ro. "He wouldn't let me watch the match! I hate him!"

Mike looked at his daughter with tired eyes. "That's enough, Rowena."

"Yeah, that's enough, Rowiener," echoed Louie.

Ro looked at Louie, then at her dad. "Why do you always take his side?" she puffed.

Gabby stormed in, holding her laptop, which dripped with orange juice. She fumed at Ro, "What did you do to my laptop? I'm going to kill you!"

"Get in line," said Uncle Gerry.

"You ruined Christmas!" screamed Gabby.

"I ruined Christmas? You ruined Christmas! All of you ruined Christmas!"

"Honey, I'm sure you don't mean that. Let's just all take a deep breath," Diane said consolingly.

Ro stared at her dad's girlfriend. "You're not in this family, Diane! Why are you even here?"

Carolina stepped in. "Do you want to get grounded on Christmas Day?"

A hard lump formed in Ro's throat. She did her best to swallow it down, but the sum of the day's chaos proved too much. "This is the worst Christmas ever!" she proclaimed.

Ro stormed out of the room. She needed to get away from everyone, so she put on her coat and headed outside.

CHAPTER
6

Ro sat by herself on the cold porch stoop, wondering how someone could be surrounded by so many people yet feel so alone. All she wanted was a good Christmas, a real Christmas, just like the ones they used to have. She took in her house, decked out with candy canes, lights, and tinsel that seemed to mock her. What was the point of festooning the house if her family ignored their Christmas traditions? She bent down, picked up the softball Mike and Louie had left behind, and chucked it at a six-foot-tall plastic lawn Santa.

"Hey, now! What gives?" said the Santa—or rather a tall, thin Black man dressed as Santa. He stepped out from behind the plastic lawn figure.

"Sorry, I didn't see you! It's been a long day,"

apologized Ro. She rubbed her nose, which was starting to get cold.

"Tell me about it. I got stuck in a chimney facedown
in Sweden. Then Rudolph's nose went out over Toronto.
Had us flying blind for a stretch."

Ro looked the gentleman up and down. She'd seen
mall Santas who more closely resembled the big jolly
guy. "Look, I know you're not really Santa. I mean, your
beard is clearly fake."

"You mean this thing? You got me on that one. I wear
it for the windburn on the sled," he said, pulling down
his fluffy fake beard to reveal a neatly trimmed goatee.

"Let me ask you something, between me and you.
Do you know anyone who has actually ever seen Santa?"
asked the man.

Ro pondered the question and shook her head. He
had a point.

"Then how do you know what he looks like? Maybe
Santa is tall and terrified of ceiling fans," said the man
with a wink.

"Look, I'm twelve. How can one guy make it across
the whole world in one night?" Ro said challengingly.

She'd had a similar conversation with the mall Santa the previous year.

"Time is a tricky thing. A lot can happen in a day," philosophized this Santa.

Ro nodded. "You can say that again. I can't wait for this day to be over."

"You hear that sound? That's the sound of someone not having a very fun Christmas. Lucky for you, Santa's here. Ho, ho, ho!" he belted out, doing his best jolly Santa impersonation. Unfortunately, all that jolliness gave him a crick in his neck. "Seriously, I think I pulled something on that one. But go ahead, give it to me. Tell me what you want."

Ro couldn't believe she was still talking to this dude. But the truth was, rando or not, he was a better listener than her family members who were huddled inside the house. "The only thing I want is for things to go back to how they used to be." A sudden breeze blew across the lawn, rustling Ro's hair.

"You mean like a do-over?" asked Santa. The wind chimes swayed as the breeze picked up speed.

"Yeah. So that this awful day never happened! So I can have a normal Christmas again!" said Ro.

The wind grew even stronger, spinning a decorative North Pole lawn sign. "Could you say that again louder? I didn't hear you," said Santa.

Ro squeezed her eyes shut, threw her hands in the air, and yelled, "I wish I could have my Christmas again!" The tension release felt good.

"That's what I thought you said," Santa replied with a smile. Ro spun around when she heard the front door creak. Carolina stepped out onto the porch.

"Ro? What are you doing out here?"

"I was talking to Tall Santa," said Ro. But when she glanced back, he was gone. Vanished. Nowhere in sight. *Weird . . .*

Carolina sighed. "Honey, what is going on with you? I understand you're having a hard time, but your behavior has been completely inappropriate."

"But he really was here," Ro tried to explain. "You've got to believe me."

"That's enough. Let's go back inside," said Carolina.

"I want you to apologize to everyone." Ro followed her mom into the house but stole a final glance at the plastic lawn Santa, hoping to find some answers. But it was just decorative. It had no wisdom for her.

CHAPTER 7

The next morning Ro awoke with a start, her alarm clock blaring a jolly rendition of "Jingle Bells" at full volume. Right. In. Her. Ear.

"Jingle bells! Jingle bells! Jingle all the way! Oh, what fun . . ."

As the song faded, an overly chipper voice chimed, "Good morning, Chicago! It's the day you've all been waiting for! It's—"

Ro slammed off the radio and sat up in bed, her head feeling foggy. "I must've hit record or something." From the side of her bed, Louie, wrapped in a ghostlike sheet, crept up. Startled, Ro jumped up and slipped on her skateboard. She crashed into the dresser, where the proud nutcracker stood. The wooden soldier wobbled from its perch, the orange juice spilled onto Gabby's laptop, and Louie removed the sheet and giggled.

"Why are you still here?" Ro asked, following Louie out of the room and down the stairs, where he Superman-leapt toward her dad.

"Gotcha, you little devil!" said Mike, wrapping the squirming boy in his arms. "Were you having fun upstairs?"

"Dad? What is happening?" Ro shook her head, trying to remember if her dad had said he and Diane were spending the night.

She heard him announce, "Guess who decided to join us."

"Morning, sleepy head," said Carolina as she chopped vegetables.

Ro walked into the kitchen, and everything was exactly the same as it had been the day before. Gabby and Diane were looking at something on Gabby's phone. "Is this a joke? We already did Christmas."

Louie ran up to Mike and stuck out his foot. "Shoelaces," he cried. Mike bent over and dutifully complied while Diane reached out toward Ro.

"Sweetie," she began, "I know it was kind of a shock having me and Louie here for Thanksgiving. But we all thought things would be easier by Christmas."

Ro's eyes widened as Diane unwrapped the last Advent calendar chocolate and popped it into her mouth. This couldn't be happening . . . *again.*

"Look what I can do," squealed Louie. He flung his feet around in some quasi tap dance moves.

Ro jumped back in shock. "I'm still dreaming. That's it."

Gabby pinched Ro hard; Ro shrieked. "Nope, definitely awake," smirked Gabby.

Ro fumbled through the next few minutes with an unshakable sense of déjà vu. *Wake up, wake up, wake up.* Abuelo Hector and Abuela Sofia arrived. Abuela peppered her cheeks with red-lipstick kisses. "Oh, my little Rowena! Did you like your sweater? I made it myself."

"All right, you'll smother the poor girl," said Abuelo Hector. "Ro, are we having a nice Christmas?"

Abuela's tummy rumbled angrily.

Ro looked at her grandma. "Abuela! You went to the greasy spoon diner again?"

"It was my fault. I should never have dragged you there," said Abuelo, dropping his keys.

Ro was crouching down to pick them up when she heard the warning grumble. "Not again," she said. But it was too late. Abuela farted, and Louie and Gabby laughed from their nearby seats. "That does it! This isn't funny," Ro insisted between dry heaves.

Ro joined her family around the tree for present opening, determined to get to the bottom of . . . well, whatever this was. This weird Christmas repeat thing. "You're all mad at me for yesterday. You're trying to teach me a lesson. Aw. Thanks, you guys. I totally get it now. I'll be so much better. I promise."

Carolina passed Ro a familiar-looking flat box. "Honey, what are you talking about? Nobody's mad at you. Here, open my present."

Ro tore the sparkling red- and silver-striped paper with feigned surprise. "A scrapbook! And paper! Wrapped in more paper."

Carolina looked hurt. "Ro, you don't have to be sarcastic."

Ro turned to her dad's girlfriend as she walked in the

room carrying a platter of cookies. "Diane, can I open your present? I've always wanted a stage makeup kit."

Ro's mom frowned. "Ro, have you been peeking at your gifts?"

"No, Mom! I swear. I can be good. I'll even like the tablet with knobs, which was probably meant for Louie, but I don't care anymore. See? I've learned my lesson. So can we all just stop with the joke now? Please?"

But the bizarro day continued. Christmas dinner, the hockey match, the shattered heirloom bowl—it was a duplicate.

Ro stumbled through the rest of her second Christmas Day. That night, she locked her bedroom door and jammed her chair against the doorknob.

CHAPTER 8

The next morning Ro awoke with a start . . . again. "Jingle Bells" blared . . . again. "This is not good," said Ro.

Downstairs, everything was exactly as it had been the two previous days.

"Guess who decided to join us," Mike said, ribbing her.

"Morning, sleepy head," said Carolina.

"Rowena, Merry Christmas," cheered Diane.

Ro racked her brain for any explanation. A simple cause. Then it hit her: Tall Santa. She had to tell her family what had happened. "I think I messed up. I wished for Christmas again. Now I'm stuck in the same day."

No one responded except for Gabby. "Crazy," she said, laughing and rolling her eyes.

"You guys don't believe me. Fine," said Ro. She headed back to her room to wait out this Christmas Day.

When Gabby knocked on her door, Ro was in bed, under a sheet fort, reviewing her top five Christmas list with a flashlight. Ro sized up Gabby, unimpressed. "Let me guess: Mom and Dad sent you to be Big Sister."

"I am your big sister. Plus I would've come on my own. Eventually. I know what you're going through." Gabby stepped into the room.

"Trust me, you have no idea," Ro assured her.

But Gabby felt she did have some idea. The divorce, Mike dating Diane, Louie coming in tow—they weren't changes Gabby had wished for. "This is hard for me, too. I may not show it the same way you do—" Gabby stopped cold. Something beneath Ro's bed had caught her eye. "My laptop."

Ro's explanation came quick, sounding equal parts desperate and apologetic. "I didn't mean to spill the juice on it! That was Louie's fault!"

"Well, lucky for you, you missed." Gabby shrugged,

holding a pristine laptop in one hand while she tucked her hair behind her ear with the other.

Ro gaped at the unblemished computer, then noticed the full glass of orange juice on her nightstand. Ro retraced her morning steps like a confused detective. "I didn't spill the juice this time. Or slip on the skateboard," she muttered to herself. She stepped over her skateboard, still nestled in its original position, on her way to her dresser, where the nutcracker still stood at attention, all in one piece. "It's like the day never happened. Everything just reset. But if everything resets . . . then nobody remembers anything! And I can change what happens. There's no consequences whatsoever. I can do whatever I want."

Gabby looked at her little sister with confusion. She had no idea what she was talking about.

Ro sat down and typed Santa an email.

Dear Santa, I really appreciate you letting me relive Christmas over and over (would've liked a little heads-up). Anywho, if I am going to be in this time loop, I'm going to have some fun!

★ ★ ★

Ro woke the next morning with a smile. "It's sledding time," she said.

A Christmas with no consequences was the most wonderful news of the year. She brainstormed all the holiday festivities she could partake in without the burden of responsibility, all the merriment she could enjoy while shunning family obligations. She bounded into the kitchen, snagged her mom's cell, and opened a rideshare app. Ro selected the most expensive, most luxurious option; why not? No consequences.

Ro waited at the curb, her sled in hand. Two kids approached. They held a homemade sign that read *Jokes 4 Charity*.

The boy spoke first. "Would you like to make a donation?"

Ro rooted her boot deeper into the snow. "You two must be new around here. How about some advice instead? See that girl over there?" She pointed across the street to a scowl-faced girl standing in front of two blow-up gingerbread man decorations. "That's Gretchen. She used to take my lunch money. Do not try to sell her a joke."

"Thanks," the kids said as they went on their way. Her neighbor, Mrs. Brown, was crossing the street when her grocery bag ripped. "My eggs!" cried the older woman. At her feet were flour, bananas, and a pool of milk. Two other neighbors, Shaun and Linda, stapled a sign to a pole for their missing cat, Cupcake. "Let us know if you see her, Ro," said Shaun.

Ro was far more interested in what rolled around the corner: a white stretch limo. This sweet rideshare was hers. Ro jumped into the backseat, noting the cushy leather interior, then looked up in surprise. "Ho, ho, ho!" said the driver.

"Tall Santa! You drive a limo, too?"

The gentleman she'd met on the lawn flashed his sparkling smile. "Oh, yeah! Santa's side hustle, baby! I also cover a tech support hotline. Speaking of which . . ." He held up his finger in the universal sign for *one moment* and answered the phone in a fake British accent. "Tech support . . . yes . . . yes . . . oh no, no, no. Have you tried restarting? Okay, I'll have to ask you to hold." Santa clicked off his headset and turned his gaze toward his passenger. "So what's the plan, Stan?"

"It's Ro. And the plan is to have Christmas like we used to."

He raised one eyebrow. "Like *we* used to. Don't you need more people for that? Like your family?"

Ro glanced back at her house. "My family is a bit too busy with other things, so I'll just have to do it for them."

First stop: Chicagoland's best sled hill. Ro had always loved her family's traditional toboggan outings. Ro's favorite runs were the ones Mike joined her on. They'd scream their heads off all the way down the bunny hill. But that was when Ro had been a kid. This Christmas, she was going it alone. And she was going for the biggie: the steepest, scariest, most advanced hill.

"Okay, Ro, you got this," she said, giving herself a little pep talk. Someone gave her a push, and her sled was off, propelling down the hill.

"AAAAAAAAAHHHH!" yelled Ro. She wasn't scared; she was petrified. She white-knuckled the sides of her sled as she rocketed down the run. But halfway down, Ro's dread turned to exhilaration, her fear to joy.

"WOO-HOOOOOOO!" she squealed. That was when Ro realized that sometimes the best way to face your fear was head-on. Just kidding: all she learned was that sledding by herself was fun.

"Watch out!" she yelled just before crashing through someone's snow fort at the base of the hill. "Sorry!"

CHAPTER 9

The next morning, "Jingle Bells" blared on Ro's radio again. She shook her head in disbelief. "Time to play!"

She hailed Tall Santa and had him deliver her straight to the number four memory on her top five Christmas list: the Pier. "Let's see how this list holds up!" she said.

Decked in shimmering snowflakes, endless tinsel, and twinkling string lights, the Pier was a winter wonderland. It was exactly what Ro needed. She delighted in the street performers, watched the bubble guy make giant bubbles, and rode the Ferris wheel (twice).

The Pier was just as good as she'd remembered. She checked it off her Christmas list.

The following morning, Ro awoke for another Christmas Day. The best part of this sudden ability to relive the same day over and over and over was she didn't have to relive it in the exact same way.

This time when Louie tried to ghost Ro, the joke was on him. Ro popped up behind him, wearing a rubber reindeer mask. "Boo!" she yelped, then chased Louie out of the room and away from the stairs, which finally allowed her to leap into her dad's arms before the tot did.

"Dad! Merry Christmas!" she yelled.

"Merry Christmas, sprout!" said Mike, grabbing Ro up in a hug. "You and Louie have fun up there?"

"I'll say. Thanks for sending him to wake me. That kid is a real delight." She and her dad entered the kitchen together.

"Guess who decided to join us," said Mike.

"Morning, sleepy head," said Carolina.

Diane smiled a little too enthusiastically. "Rowena! Merry Christmas!"

"Diane! Merry Christmas to you!" Ro pulled in her

dad's girlfriend for what seemed like a warm embrace, then whispered low in Diane's ear, "Hand over the chocolate, lady, and nobody gets hurt."

Stunned, Diane opened her palm, revealing the last Advent calendar chocolate—yet uneaten. Ro grabbed it, popped it into her mouth, and chewed happily. "Mmm. I'm getting notes of cinnamon. And a hint of victory."

"Abuela!" Ro said, greeting her grandparents. She pulled Abuela into a hug and whispered, "We haven't opened presents yet, but between you and me, I love the sweater."

Abuela covered Ro's forehead with kisses. Abuelo Hector stepped up and put his arms around his beloved granddaughter. "All right, you'll smother the poor girl. Ro, are we—"

"Having a wonderful Christmas, Abuelo. Thank you for asking," Ro said, smiling, as she knocked the keys from her grandfather's hands and kicked them toward Gabby and Louie. "Oops . . ." she smirked. "Gabby, could you be a dear and pick those up?" Ro spun Abuela toward Gabby and Louie just as Gabby bent over to retrieve the keys. She farted in Gabby's and Louie's faces. Yup, Ro was definitely having a more wonderful Christmas this time around.

At gift-opening time, Ro targeted the presents she knew contained chocolate, plucking her favorite candies from each box before discarding the rest.

"How did she know which boxes have the chocolates?" wondered a bemused Uncle Gerry.

"That's easy," said Ro. "I'm psychic."

"Ha. Funny, Ro," Uncle Gerry responded.

"You're the one taking the comedy class, Uncle Gerry," Ro quipped.

Gerry looked at Bruce accusingly. "You told them?"

"Who wants to open presents?" offered Carolina.

Ro's hand shot into the air. "Yay! Let's do it, Mom. I can't wait for my new scrapbook. Or how about a makeup kit, Diane? Because you know me so well. And gee, Dad, I'd sure love that glove, but Louie switched the tags, so I guess I'll settle for a tablet with knobs." Ro continued as her family stood agape. "Do you believe me now? Or do you need more proof?"

Carolina stared down her daughter. "Rowena, that's enough." But her disapproval was drowned out by the rest of the family's shouts for more psychic proof.

Ro obliged. "Okay, first I'll need to ask a few questions. Dad, how much cash do you have in your pocket?"

"Sixty-two dollars? And ten cents," said Mike, counting.

"And Uncle Gerry, what color is your underwear?"

"My underwear?"

"Just answer the question," said Ro, her arms flapping by her sides.

"Light blue."

"I'd say more a robin's-egg blue," clarified Uncle Bruce. "Would've been the same answer yesterday," he revealed.

"Abuela, who was your first crush?"

Hector laughed. "You don't need psychic powers for that one, mijita. That would be . . ."

"Antonio Diego," Sofia said in a dreamy voice. "He had these green eyes the color of an old nickel. And hair like a horse."

Ro continued around the room. "Diane, you're so good with dogs. Did you ever have one?"

Mike cleared his throat and crossed his arms. "Ro, where are you going with this?"

But Diane didn't mind. "I think it's nice Rowena wants to learn more about us. And, yes, I did have a dog once. His name was Biscuit. He was this adorable little French bulldog and I loved him so very much." Diane began to tear up. "One day I left a bag of chips lying around. And then I couldn't find him. And I went all over the house yelling, 'Biscuit—'"

"Okay, Ro, I think that's plenty," interrupted Mike.

"You're right, Dad," agreed Ro. She had everything she needed. "See y'all next time," she said, then sauntered upstairs to her room. The next day's Christmas was going to be even better.

CHAPTER 10

Christmas Again. This morning, ghost Louie was greeted by another sheet ghost.

"That's good, Rowena," Louie said, giggling. But when he pulled down the sheet to reveal Rowena, it collapsed on the floor in a heap. There was no one in it. It was a real ghost! Louie screamed and ran as Ro, snickering, peeked out from behind the bathroom door. In her hands was a fishing pole with a line connected to the "ghost."

A little while later, the "Amazing Rowena" joined her family in the living room to shock them with her psychic might. "Sixty-two dollars and ten cents," guessed Ro as Mike counted the money in his pocket. He looked up in wonder; she was correct to the penny.

Ro turned to Uncle Gerry. "Light blue . . . er, the color of your underwear. But Bruce thinks it's more of a robin's egg. Either way, you should do your laundry."

Uncle Gerry glowered. "I am very busy!"

Ro continued her act. "And, Abuela? I'm glad you chose Abuelo over Antonio Diego." Abuela gasped. "Besides, it's only hair."

"Horse hair Antonio?" questioned Abuelo.

"Oh, and, Diane," continued Ro, "Biscuit says hi."

Diane's face fell. "Biscuit?"

"Yeah. The little French bulldog sitting next to you. He's got a bag of chips in his mouth. And he's not too happy about you holding Olive."

Diane set down Bruce and Gerry's dog just as Bruce fashioned a hat out of silver foil wrapping paper. "You're not getting in here," he said, placing it on his head.

Uncle Gerry leaned in toward his partner. "Can I get one of those?"

Ro found the whole scene terribly amusing.

CHAPTER 11

Time continued to loop for Ro: wake up, "Jingle Bells," Christmas Day, repeat. "Time to spice things up," Ro said. On this Christmas, Rowena asked Tall Santa to drive her to the hockey rink. She jumped out of the limo and looked up at the marquee, which read *Annual Santas vs. Elves Match*. She was about to check off number three on her best Christmas ever list.

The rink was full and the crowds were rowdy. Ro sat in the packed stadium stands, quite happy to be among the like-minded fans who chose their team over their family on Christmas. Unfortunately, her team was struggling to find a gap in the Elves' defense. "Come on, Santas!" She raised her fist in the air. "Throw some elbows! Get naughty."

"Boy, the Santas look sluggish out there," bellowed Hosea Sanders over the loudspeaker. "That's what they get for eating cookies all night."

Ro winced as the Elves stole the puck and took it coast to coast.

Elves fans roared; Santas fans groaned. "I'm gonna need more snacks."

On her way to the concession stand, Ro passed the game announcers congratulating a young couple. They stood in front of a life-size glass snowman. It was filled with mini candy canes.

"So how does it feel to win a thousand dollars?" asked Hosea, his voice just as deep in person as it was over the PA system.

The woman gushed. "We can visit my parents in Florida! This is the best Christmas ever!"

As the crowd around the couple applauded, Ro asked, "Excuse me. Did they just win a thousand dollars?"

"That's right. They guessed the closest number of candy canes in that snowman and won the raffle," said announcer Israel Idonije.

"What was the winning number?" Ro asked, smiling

'Twas the night before Christmas when Rowena Clybourne shared her Top 5 Christmas Memories list with her mom, Carolina.

Christmas morning didn't get off to a great start when Ro was woken up by a ghost, who turned out to be Louie, the son of Ro's dad's girlfriend.

Ro chased Louie down the stairs, but he sought protection in the arms of Ro's dad, Mike.

Ro wanted Christmas to be like it used to, which didn't include Mike's girlfriend, Diane.

It started to feel a little more like Christmas when Ro's grandparents arrived.

Mike and Diane had the perfect present for Ro, but her and Louie's gifts got switched.

Ro's grandparents gave Carolina a family treasure, but it broke when Uncle Bruce slipped on Ro's crumpled wrapping paper.

The day got worse when Ro demolished the Christmas decorations while trying to retrieve the TV remote from Louie.

Before Christmas Day was done, Ro made a wish with Tall Santa for a Christmas do-over.

Once Ro realized she was stuck in a time loop, she decided to have some fun. First stop: sledding!

Ro dressed like Clara to sneak into *The Nutcracker* department store window.

Ro also stopped at the Hancock Center to conquer her fears on the "platform thingy."

Ro cheered on the Santas at the Santas versus Elves hockey match.

Ro even joined the Santas on the ice to help them score the winning goal.

Ro's older sister, Gabby, helped her see that she had new Christmas memories to make.

Once Ro realized that Christmas was about spending time with the ones you love, she had a very merry Christmas.

and thinking of just how many concessions she could buy the next day with a grand. She rubbed her hands together. If she was going to repeat Christmas, she might as well do it in style.

★ ★ ★

Ro returned to the ice rink the next day. This time, she headed straight for the candy cane–filled snowman and placed her guess. "Seventeen thousand five hundred and thirty-six. Nine thousand are red. Eight thousand five hundred and thirty-six green."

Hosea checked Ro's answer against the winning number, startled to see she'd hit the bull's-eye. "So what are you going to do with your money?" Hosea asked, handing Ro a thick envelope stuffed with cash. Ro knew exactly what she'd do: have some holiday fun!

★ ★ ★

On her next Christmas, Ro sponged up every nook of Chicago's Museum of Science and Industry. Without her family, Ro ran unhindered from one hall to the next. She survived tornados in the *Science Storms* exhibit.

She toured the miniature fairy castle. But she saved her favorite exhibit for last: *Christmas Around the World.* The number five memory on her top five list, it show-cased Christmas customs from forty cultures around the globe. At the center of the majestic exhibit stood the four-story-tall Grand Tree, which made Ro smile most of all. It was the one she and Gabby had posed in front of years before. She sat beneath it and imagined how families around the world were all enjoying their annual holiday traditions together at that very moment. The idea of it warmed her heart—even as she enjoyed her family's tradition all by herself.

★ ★ ★

On her next day of Christmas, Ro visited the aquarium. Nothing like visiting the penguins to get you in the Christmas spirit.

Then she decided to hit number two on her list: the "platform thingy" at the top of the John Hancock Center. She waited patiently in line, determined to conquer her fear. But one step onto the platform, Ro's knees turned weak and her breath caught short, and she ran toward the exit without taking her turn. Eh, she'd find the nerve to enjoy the platform thingy some other Christmas Day. One thing Ro knew for sure: she wasn't running out of Christmases anytime soon. It took three Christmases, but Ro conquered her fear and managed to enjoy the platform thing. In fact, it was awesome. She even wrote Santa to tell him about it.

Hey Santa, I never thought I would be able to do the big platform thingy. I guess with enough practice you can do anything and make things happen the way you want them to.

The first two weeks of her Christmas loop, Ro ran through every item on her top five list. Then she spent the next two weeks doubling back and raising the ante. No Christmas consequences was this kid's dream.

She bundled up in her down coat, wool scarf, and pom-pom beanie and strolled down Chicago's famed State Street. Its storefronts were famous for their extravagant holiday window displays packed with animatronic puppets and jaw-dropping artistry. Mike and Carolina used to take her and Gabby to see them every year. Ro's favorite were the *Nutcracker* windows. She was enthralled by the tale of the bold girl who braved a fantastic Christmas adventure. Ro stopped in front of the windows; they looked just as they had when she was a kid. Clara, the Sugar Plum Fairy, the Mouse King—they were all there in their glittery glory.

Ro revisited the State Street department store window displays on her next Christmas. But this time, Ro dressed as Clara, found her way inside the dazzling *Nutcracker* display, and danced alongside the animatronic Sugar Plum Fairy. She almost got busted when Mike, Diane, and Louie walked by, but she managed to duck out before her dad returned for a double take.

Ro returned to the hockey rink on several Christmases. First she suited up in a Santas jersey. The next time, she scrounged up the nerve to play beside her heroes. She worked the ice, evaded the Elves with some slick stickhandling, and even heard the announcer comment, "Check out the hands on little Santa!"

After multiple Christmases skating with the team,

Ro commanded the ice. With five seconds left in a tie game, she drove wide past a defender, curled on a dime, and shot the puck into the net just as time expired. Team Santa hoisted Ro on their shoulders and paraded around the rink. Ro wondered if Mike was watching the game on TV, if he'd seen her score the buzzer beater. She guessed not; he was probably outside playing catch with Louie. Oh, well. It was still pretty cool.

With each passing Christmas, Ro sought out more joy. But no matter how she spent Christmas—how many fears she conquered, festivities she attended, and adventures she experienced—Christmas at home unfolded the same way. Louie and Diane were still there, her parents were still divorced, and family traditions still fell by the wayside.

On Christmas Day thirty, Rowena's family set up for a game of What's That?

"Hey, Ro! We're playing What's That? You can be on our team," sang Carolina, eager for Ro to join family game night.

"It wouldn't be fair," said Ro. After all, she'd already watched this game play out more than a few times.

"Sweetie, it's just a fun game. None of us are very good, except for Gabby."

Abuelo Hector snored, and everyone laughed. In fact, her abuela was asleep, too.

"Same time every Christmas," said Gerry. "Don't worry. Bruce and I'll bring them up to your room after this."

"You mean after we finish kicking your butts?" Bruce said challengingly.

Carolina grabbed a black marker. "We'll see about that, buddy. All right, it's my turn. Rowena, sit."

Ro plopped down next to her teammates, Gabby and Gerry, as Carolina stepped up to the easel. She selected the top card from the colorful stack.

"You got this, Mom!" cheered Gabby.

"Come on, Lina! You can do it!" Gerry said.

"And . . . go!" shouted Mike, starting the timer.

Carolina drew a circle.

"Planet," Ro said, devoid of enthusiasm.

"Yes! Good guess, honey," gushed Carolina as she selected her next card. She read the clue, then started her drawing with a single diagonal line.

"Sail," pronounced Ro.

"Wow, th-that's also correct," stammered Carolina.

Ro yawned. Carolina flipped the next card, but before she could start to draw, Ro guessed, "Toast."

Her mom nodded in disbelief and flipped to the next card.

"Frog," said Ro before Carolina's marker even touched paper.

"Bow tie," Ro said before Carolina could finish reading the next card. This went on for several more cards.

Everyone stared at Ro in shock. "Can we trade Louie for Ro?" asked Bruce.

But all Ro wanted to do was trade this Christmas for a past one—one when her parents were still married. She wanted a Christmas filled with beloved traditions, like Winterfest and sledding. There had to be a way to bring the past back.

CHAPTER 12

Christmas Day thirty-one. Ro exited her house and looked across the street to find Gretchen taking the fundraising money.

The boy lunged for the container. Gretchen stuck out her boot and tripped him, laughing as he fell into an inflatable lawn gingerbread man. His sister helped him up.

Ro shook her head at the scene. "Can't say I didn't warn 'em."

Then she heard a familiar crash and glanced at Mrs. Brown. "My eggs!" cried the elderly woman. Behind Mrs. Brown, a couple stapled a flyer on a post: *Cupcake: Missing Cat.*

Ro paid no mind to any of it. She hopped into Tall Santa's limo, directed him to take her to the hockey arena, and headed straight for the concession stand run by costumed elves. "One hot chocolate, please. And don't skimp on the marshmallows." Ro plunked down cash, looked up, then stepped back in surprise. "Tall Santa! Weren't you just driving the limo?"

Tall Santa, with a goofy green elf hat perched on his head, grinned. "As you can see, I'm a man of many hats. Even funny little elf hats that tend to make my head itch." He started whipping up Ro's order. "Is your family meeting you here?"

Ro tugged at the wrists of her hoodie. "They're too busy. But I pretty much know everyone here, so it's almost like family. Isn't that right, Frankie?" Ro nodded at the girl behind her in line. The girl, weirded out, walked off. Ro shrugged. "She's just nervous 'cause she's proposing to her boyfriend at Winterfest tonight."

Santa added steaming milk to the cocoa. "Aw, that's sweet."

"Too bad an ornament is gonna fall from the tree and shatter her moment," Ro said, laughing.

"Oh, that's not too sweet. Why don't you give her a little heads-up?" asked Santa.

Ro glanced at him sideways. "I've been busy. I'm reliving my favorite Christmas memories."

"Fun. I'll give you that, but aren't some of those favorite Christmas memories involving your family?"

"Well, yeah. But I dunno, Santa. Everything's different this year. My dad brought his girlfriend and her little boy, who is a nightmare. Things just aren't the same with my family."

"I hear you. You know, once upon a time the North Pole was a quiet little place. Back when it was just me and Mrs. Claus, and Dasher and Dancer. Smash cut to today and we've got nine hungry reindeer and a thousand noisy elves. My point is, families change. What's important is you're all still together on Christmas."

Ro grimaced. "But I don't want my family to change. And Christmas was so much better before Mom and Dad split."

Santa loaded up Ro's cocoa with marshmallows,

checking it twice to make sure they were stacked securely. "Maybe so. But while you're running around trying to relive the past, think of all the great new memories you're missing out on. Besides, Ro, they'll always be your mom and dad, even if they're not together."

Ro's eyes brightened. Tall Santa was a genius. She should have listened to him thirty Christmases earlier. She'd been approaching the whole repeat experience the wrong way. "Why didn't I think of this sooner? I can get Mom and Dad back together!"

Tall Santa stared, stupefied. "That's your takeaway from all of this?"

"Yes! This could solve everything!" Ro couldn't believe it had taken her that long to realize why she'd been repeating Christmas. All she had to do to escape the infinite time loop was help her parents reconcile.

Santa set down Ro's drink with an air of defeat. "One hot chocolate, extra marshmallows."

"Thanks, Tall Santa!" cheered Ro. But when she looked up, he'd vanished.

CHAPTER
13

Ro awoke on her next Christmas and launched Operation: Rekindle. Once her parents got back together, family Christmas would return to what it used to be.

She got to work on her plan first thing. Carolina was in the kitchen, prepping Christmas dinner. Ro climbed up on the counter as her mom rolled dough. Ro swung her legs as she talked.

"Hey, Mom? If you had to pick one Christmas to live over again, which would it be?"

Carolina kneaded a ball of dough. "That's interesting. Why do you ask?"

"Just wondering. If you had to, which Christmas would you relive?"

Carolina paused for a moment, then smiled, as if retrieving a long-lost memory from a vault. "Well, my favorite Christmas would be your first Christmas."

"My first Christmas?" Ro leaned in. Ro's mom told her all about the big Christmas party they had planned.

"We spent two days getting the place together," Carolina recalled. "We didn't have much furniture. But we had a tree and Christmas lights. A wreath for the door. And these horrible ugly matching Christmas sweatshirts."

Ro chuckled at the thought of her parents going twinsies. She couldn't believe there had been a point in time when they dressed alike—on purpose.

Ro asked her dad the same question and got the same answer. "You were nine months old," he recalled. "It was also our first Christmas here. Your mom and I planned a party.

"Then, of course, nobody could come."

"Why not?" asked Ro. She'd never heard the story before and loved how young and in love her parents had been.

Mike gesticulated wildly as he told Ro about the big snowstorm that had come in out of nowhere. "Snowed in the whole block," he recalled. "We lost power. No TV or lights. Fortunately, your mom kept a box of candles. We lit every single one. And it was just . . . spectacular. Wish you could remember it, Ro."

Mike had a far-off look in his eye as he relived the magical moment. "The whole house smelled like sandalwood. I built a fire, and your mom and I sat drinking hot cocoa and telling stories while Gabriela played with her toys and you crawled around on the rug like a little crocodile. It was just the four of us then. Things were so much simpler."

What Ro noticed most of all was that both her parents ended the story the same way, saying, "Those were great times."

Ro knew what she had to do. For the first time in a long while, she looked forward to waking up on Christmas Day again. She was going to re-create her first Christmas and rekindle her parents' relationship.

★ ★ ★

On her next Christmas, Ro lay awake in bed long before her clock radio could blare "Jingle Bells." She made a checklist of everything she had to get done that day, and it started with Diane. Her dad's new girlfriend definitely wasn't present at Ro's first Christmas, which meant she couldn't be around today.

"First things first, let's get rid of any distractions," said Ro. Remembering Diane's cat allergies, Ro grabbed Diane's coat from the hook, then marched into the backyard in search of her neighbors' lost cat. "Here, kitty, kitty. Come here, Cupcake. Come here, Cupcake. I know you're around here somewhere. Here's some yummy, yummy tuna, Cupcake."

A line of paw prints in the snow led Ro to the far bushes. She cracked open a can of tuna, set it atop Diane's coat, and watched the cat emerge from the shadows, following the scent. "There you are, you little runaway," said Ro.

Cupcake stretched out on Diane's coat, rubbing her fur against the wool as she devoured the fish. Then Ro heard a chorus of additional tiny meows in the bushes.

Ro smiled. "I'm gonna need more tuna!"

A short while later, Diane threw on her coat as

she headed outside to watch Louie play catch on the lawn. Within moments, she was sneezing, sniffling, and splotchy.

"Diane? Are you okay?" asked Mike.

"Achoo!" was her only response.

Once she was inside again, her nose was flaring up like Rudolph's. She took some medicine and went to rest in the guest room.

"One down. Three to go," smirked Ro. Next up? Her uncles. They hadn't been at her first Christmas. She had to get them out of the house, too, and she knew just how to do it: Olive. Ro lured Olive up to her room, then called her Uncle Gerry on his phone.

"Hello, am I speaking to Olive's daddy?" she asked in a disguised voice. "I found this adorable little dog and her tag says her name is Olive. . . ."

Bruce grabbed their keys, scarves, and hats, and the uncles jumped in their car to go pick up Olive, who had "run away."

Ro's brilliant strategy was about to enter phase three. "Where have you been?" Carolina asked as Ro hurried down the stairs to join them.

Ro shrugged innocently. "Playing. Where is everybody?"

"Diane's asleep in the guest room. And your uncles went to get Olive. The little stinkball ran off this morning and got an hour outta town," said Mike.

"Poor thing," said Ro.

"Thankfully, your grandparents are still around," added Carolina. "Hey, can you help me finish the dishes?" she asked Mike.

"And the grandparents will be asleep by What's That?—which leaves only one . . ." Ro said to herself. She beckoned Louie into the second-floor bathroom. "You wanna see something cool?" she asked him.

"But why do we have to be in here?" he asked as Ro directed Louie to the bathtub, with a laptop, headphones, and a pillow.

"Because it's the best reception in the whole house. Observe." With a few clicks, Ro opened a video app. "You can watch anything you want."

"Whoa . . . even scary things? Like a shark ripping off a man's head. And the man comes back as a zombie and eats the shark!"

"I like your vision. Let's see what we can find." Ro ran a search, brought up several scary videos on the screen, strapped headphones onto Louie, and clicked play.

"But Mom says if I watch scary things, I'll have bad dreams."

Ro cocked her head, a knowing expression on her face. "Something tells me you'll forget everything by morning."

With Louie distracted, it was time to execute the final step. Ro tiptoed into the garage and made her way to the fuse box. She pushed the fuse handle down and the lights throughout the entire house cut off. Total blackout. Ro stood in the dark, feeling proud that her scheme was underway.

★ ★ ★

The family room looked different by candlelight; the dozen flickering flames scattered throughout bathed it in a warm, romantic hue. Carolina lit the last candle as Mike walked in. "Just got off the phone with the electric company. They can't send anyone until morning."

"Makes sense. It's Christmas," said Carolina.

"On the bright side," said Mike, "place looks great with all these candles."

"It was Ro's idea. Kinda reminds me . . ."

"Of our first Christmas here?" said Mike, finishing his ex's sentence. "I was thinking the same thing."

Ro entered, carrying two piping hot mugs. Her face had a goofy smile. "I made hot cocoas! Mom, Dad, sit, enjoy yourselves. You've both earned it. Love you."

Mike took a quick sip as Ro sauntered out of the room. It couldn't have gone better if she had planned it, which she had.

"Where is everybody?" asked Gabby, sneaking up on Ro, who was peering at her parents around the corner.

"Shhh! Mom and Dad are having a moment. It's working." Mike and Carolina were seated on the same couch, their eyes sparkling in the dancing candlelight. They shared a wholehearted laugh.

Gabby eyed her younger sister with suspicion. "What are you doing?"

Ro leaned in to catch another glimpse of her parents together, her face alight with joy. "I'm making Mom and

Dad fall in love again. All they needed was some time to themselves."

"Ugh, you can be such a baby. Mom and Dad aren't getting back together. You need to accept that."

Ro's hope remained unshaken. "And you need to have a little faith. Observe." She unwound a fishing line, which was attached to a complex system of pulleys and sprockets. Ro tugged it, and the chain of gears lowered two silver bells above her parents' heads. Attached to the bells was a small green sprig.

Mike spoke, not yet noticing. "Lina, I know today couldn't have been easy. Are you sure it's okay if we sleep over?"

"What am I gonna do, kick you out now? I'm kidding. Besides, I think it's good for the girls to see us all getting along. Especially on Christmas."

That was Ro's cue. "Let the smooching begin." She yanked the fishing wire. The bells chimed, causing her parents to glance up.

"Is that mistletoe?" asked Mike.

Carolina's eyes narrowed. "Why do I have the feeling we're being watched?"

Mike and Carolina puckered up and leaned in, cutting the space between them to almost nothing. Then Mike kissed Carolina . . . on the cheek.

The wide grin on Ro's face evaporated. "That's it? That can't be it."

"You're a real cupid," Gabby said, sassing her. She hip checked Ro and rounded the corner into the family room, where Mike spotted her.

"Gabby-pie! Did you put up this mistletoe?"

"Nope. That would be—"

"Rowena!" shouted both her parents at once.

"This might be harder than I thought," Ro sighed.

CHAPTER 14

Ro spent her next Christmas on a fact-finding mission. If Operation: Rekindle was going to work, she'd need more information. She stood on the front lawn, ready to play catch with Louie and Mike.

"Hey, Dad? Some kids in my school are going steady. They even brag about having their own song."

"Do kids still say 'going steady'?"

"Bear with me, Dad. I'm trying to speak in terms you relate to. Anyway, did you and Mom have a song?"

"We had a wedding song."

"Really? What song?" Ro adjusted her glove. Now she was getting somewhere.

Later, Ro joined Carolina in the kitchen, hoping her

mom would fill in any relationship blanks. "What was Dad like when you were first married? What was it you liked about him?"

"Well, he was always handy," she told her daughter. "He designed this house, you know. Anytime anything needed fixing, he was there. I always thought it was very impressive."

Now that was information Ro could work with. When Carolina left the kitchen for a minute, Ro opened the fridge and grabbed as many items as she could carry. She stuffed it all—carrots, celery, sardines, pickles, a leftover sandwich—into the garbage disposal. Seconds later, it made a glorious screeching clunk and came to a halt. Now all she had to do was find her dad to fix it. She was sure it would make sparks fly between her parents.

A few minutes later, Mike lay under the sink, his legs sticking out into the kitchen. He held out his hand; Carolina passed him a wrench as if it was the most natural thing in the world. Mike let out a few grunts, turned the wrench, and popped up. "What are you guys eating?" he asked. "That should do it. Merry Christmas."

He switched on the disposal. The sink gurgled, then exploded, drenching Mike with its soggy contents.

Carolina tried not to laugh, but she couldn't help it. "You might want to take a shower?" she asked.

While Mike showered, Ro went out to the garage in search of something special! She left what she had found outside the bathroom door with a note that read *Thanks for all your help. See you by the fire. Love, C.*

Next Ro retrieved the theater makeup kit Diane had given her. "I was wondering if you could be my model," she said to her mom.

"Ro, I still have so much to do."

"This was my present from Diane. I wanted to show her how much I appreciate her gift."

"Aw, that's nice, honey."

"It'll only take a second. I promise," Ro said with a smile. Her mom was a natural beauty, but this was a special occasion. And after cooking in the kitchen all day and staying up late the night before, wrapping presents, Carolina looked a touch tired. Nothing a little lipstick and mascara couldn't fix. After ten minutes, Ro stepped back.

"How do I look?" asked Carolina.

Ro held up a hand mirror; Carolina and her daughter both recoiled. Ro tried to soften the blow. "The important thing is, how do you feel?"

"Like I escaped from the circus," Carolina said, frowning.

"Guess that answers both questions," said Ro. So that day's makeover wasn't going to change Mike's heart. But the next day's?

★ ★ ★

Ro spent the following Christmas Day watching online makeup tutorials. By the Christmas Day after that, she was the Michelangelo of makeup artists. Her hands twirled around Carolina's face. She knew when to use a small dot of concealer and where to land a well-placed illuminator. Carolina sat in awe of her daughter's previously unknown talent.

"Where did you learn all this stuff?"

"It's makeup, Mom, not rocket science. Now hold still so I can finish contouring your nose."

"I like my nose."

"I do, too. We're just enhancing what's already there. And voilà!"

Carolina looked like herself, just more youthful and glowing. Her eyes looked wide, her lips full, her cheeks dewy.

While Carolina admired her makeover, Ro added one last touch of glam, spritzing her mom with perfume. They both coughed. Okay, maybe that was just a bit too much.

Ro headed to the garage. She tugged on the fuse box handle, and the house went pitch-black. It was showtime.

★ ★ ★

In the family room, Carolina hummed to herself as she lit candles. She tugged on the sleeves of the ugly Christmas sweatshirt that Ro had dug up in the garage. She hadn't remembered it being so itchy.

Mike walked in. "Just got off the phone with the—" He stopped short and laughed.

"Ro gave you one, too?" Carolina smiled, pointing at his matching sweater.

"I can't believe you still have these."

Despite looking ridiculous, both Mike and Carolina enjoyed the fond memories that were woven into the sweatshirts.

Ro watched her parents from the hallway and smiled. And when Gabby appeared, Ro was prepared.

"Where is everybody?" Gabby asked predictably.

Ro fanned out a fat stack of cash. "It's yours if you help me."

Gabby was not one to go along with her sister's schemes, but she'd had her eye on a set of high-end earbuds, so she made an exception.

As before, the sisters eavesdropped on their parents' conversation.

"Well, aside from the power outage, sneezing fits, and a dog disappearance, today wasn't a total disaster. On the bright side, place looks great with all these candles," offered Mike.

Carolina wrapped her hands around her mug, taking in its warmth. "It was Ro's idea. Kinda reminds me . . ."

"Of our first Christmas here? I was thinking the same thing."

That was the girls' cue. Ro and Gabby blasted music and ran into the room. "Mom! Dad! We wanna dance! Come on!" Gabby took her mom's hand. Ro bopped toward Mike, who embraced her, then twirled her around until she grew dizzy. The foursome switched partners, Ro spinning with Gabby, Mike dancing with Carolina.

The sight of her parents dancing together filled Ro with a happiness she'd long been missing. Everything felt right again. Ro and Gabby snuck out of the room as a slower ballad began to play. Mike and Carolina shifted effortlessly into a slow dance.

"My gosh. I used to love this song," said Carolina. She tilted her head back the way she always did when she was relaxed and at ease.

"I'd hope so. You picked it for our wedding," said Mike.

"That's right! I did! I've got good taste."

Ro's smile stretched. She tapped on a remote, and a ceiling fan turned on, giving Carolina's hair a subtle, romantic windswept effect. But then the fan ramped up to turbo speed, spinning out of control, blasting away Carolina with a mighty gust.

"What is happening to this place?" asked Mike. He finally got the fan to shut off.

Carolina sat down on the couch. "Well, turns out the house is still a work in progress, even after all these years. Too bad we can't find the genius who designed it. Oh, wait . . ."

"Touché," said Mike as he sat down with her.

In the hallway, Ro tugged on her fishing line pulley system, ringing the silver bells that hung above her parents.

"Is that mistletoe?" asked Mike.

Carolina peered around. "Why do I have the feeling we're being watched?"

"Girls!" shouted both parents at once.

"You know, I feel bad taking your money," said Gabby, "but not bad enough not to take it."

Ro tried to pinpoint what had gone wrong. Her parents had been laughing and dancing and . . . well, had been themselves again. "But they're supposed to kiss.

They're supposed to fall in love! Things are supposed to go back to how they used to be!"

Gabby looked at Ro sympathetically. "Ro, that's never going to happen. It doesn't matter what you do."

But Ro knew that it did matter what she did. If she just got it right one of these Christmases, her folks would fall back in love.

"Dad's getting remarried," said Gabby.

A high-pitched tone pierced through Ro's head, and the world around her blurred. "You're lying. It's not true."

A few minutes later, Ro sat on the couch between her parents.

Mike spoke first. "It is true, sprout. I asked Diane to marry me. She said yes."

Ro felt buried beneath the weight of her shock and hurt. "Why didn't anybody tell me?"

Mike took his daughter's hand. "Honey, we wanted to. Our plan was to wait until the new year."

"Why?"

"Because we didn't want to ruin your Christmas."

Ro tried to swallow the rock-hard lump in her throat

and fight back the tears that started trickling down her cheeks.

"Rowena, honey, it's gonna be okay."

"But I miss our family. I miss the way it used to be."

"I know you do, sweetie," said Carolina. "And it's okay to be sad. But we all love you. And this just means our family is growing and there'll be even more people who love you."

Ro had heard enough. "I don't want more people to love me." She stormed up the stairs and slammed her bedroom door, swearing this was her worst Christmas Day yet.

CHAPTER 15

On her next Christmas Day, Ro didn't get out of bed. Why bother? Her dad was getting remarried, her family would never be the same, and Christmas would always be ruined. There was nothing she could do about it. When Carolina finally stuck her head in, Ro was under the covers, reading Dickens's *A Christmas Carol*.

"Merry Christmas, sleepy head. Don't you want to get up? Run a brush through your hair?"

Ro did not. "Why, Mom? What's the point?" She went back to reading about Scrooge and his ghosts.

"Because it's Christmas? And you're a kid? What are you reading?"

"*A Christmas Carol*. It's about this guy Ebenezer.

Everyone's giving him a hard time, but he's not so bad. He just wants things to be the way they always were."

Carolina sat on the edge of Ro's bed. "Is that what it's about? Sounds like you need to keep reading." Ro buried her face back in the book. Carolina smirked. "Not right this minute! Your father and Diane are here. So get your butt downstairs. Vamos."

Ro complied, sort of. Wearing sunglasses and a bathrobe over her pajamas, she ambled into the kitchen with attitude to spare.

Mike looked up and took in her tousled appearance. "Guess who decided to join us."

Ro darted straight to the freezer, pulled out a tub of ice cream, and started shoveling it into her mouth. Mike and Diane traded looks.

"Everything okay, sprout?" Mike asked.

"Just great, Dad. It's Christmas. The gift that keeps on giving." She squeezed cookie dough from a roll into her mouth, followed it with a spray of whipped cream, and washed it down with a gulp of eggnog straight from the carton. Then she burped as her family watched in horror.

Ro didn't care—about any of it. No matter what she tried to change, she ended up where she started: on Christmas morning, with parents who were never, ever getting back together.

Her family gathered joyfully under the tree, unwrapping gifts and exchanging stories, but Ro continued to sulk. She picked up the tablet with knobs and started to draw.

"Does anyone else see this? Ro is doing the *Mona Lisa*," marveled Abuelo Hector.

"Yeah, Hector, I'm sure it's great," said Mike sarcastically.

Ro held up the screen to show her family a perfect replica of the *Mona Lisa*. Everyone gasped.

"I'm out," said Ro, handing Louie the tablet as she exited the room. Louie shook the tablet to clear the masterpiece from the screen before anyone could stop him.

Ro was officially over Christmas Again. She spent her

next couple of Christmases trying to destroy the alarm clock that signaled the start of this day-on-repeat.

The next time her family gathered in the living room opening presents, Ro tried to get out of the house.

"Ro? Come here. Don't you want to open your gifts?" Carolina asked.

"Yeah, sprout, what's the matter?" asked Mike.

Ro paused, her eyes filled with despair. Her voice resonated with defeat. "I just don't believe in it anymore."

"You don't believe in what, sweetie?" asked Diane.

"I don't believe in Christmas."

"Louie, cover your ears," Diane said.

An audible gasp reverberated throughout the house.

Ro loved Christmas. Christmas was her jam. She believed in the magic. And yet here she stood, deflated and most unjolly.

"Rowena, you don't mean that," said Abuela Sofia. "Christmas is the most wonderful time of year."

"Is it, Abuela? Really? What's so wonderful about it?"

Gabby knew the answer to that one. "Um. Presents? Duh."

Uncle Bruce chimed in. "Yeah, Ro. What about presents?"

"Uncle Bruce, do you even remember what you got me last year?" Ro said challengingly.

"Sure I do. It was a . . . um . . ." He looked to Uncle Gerry for help, but his partner shrugged, clueless.

"I'm sure I loved it," said Ro. "But I can't remember what it was, either. None of us need these presents, so what's the point of doing this every year?"

Carolina smiled at her daughter. "Honey, it's not about the presents. It's the thought behind them."

"And what about all the other great things about Christmas, like Christmas trees?" asked Gerry.

Ro observed the tree, smothered in ornaments and tinsel, anchored to a stand, forced to wear a tree skirt. "Look at this tree, Uncle Gerry. If you really think about it, it's probably sad. One day it was in the woods, minding its own business. Then some jerk comes along and chops it down. Now it's in our house and we've covered it with lights and festive decorations. How would you like if someone brought you into the house and covered you with festive decorations?"

"I wouldn't like it. Not one bit," Louie said.

Finally she agreed with the little shrimp about something. "Thank you, Louie. Face it, you guys. Christmas is overrated." Ro walked out of the room, leaving everyone bummed in her unmerry Christmas wake.

CHAPTER 16

Ro needed to locate Tall Santa. That guy seemed to be everywhere until you needed him; then he was nowhere to be found. Not in the limo, not on her lawn, not at the hockey rink. Ro put Gabby's stolen laptop to good use. She composed a letter to Tall Santa.

Hey, Big Guy, I know we haven't chatted in a minute, but I could really use your help. Thanks for the Christmas wish. It's been a lot of fun. But can you please make it stop now?

Your friend,
Rowena

Sealed envelope in hand, Gabby rushed into Carolina's office. "Hey, Mom, can we mail this to the North Pole?"

Carolina was pleased to see her daughter still believed in sending Santa letters. "Honey, the post office is closed today, but we can mail it tomorrow."

Tomorrow? Ro knew there was no such thing as tomorrow. She ran around the house screaming, "Noooooooooooooooooo."

Finally, Ro marched up to the plastic lawn Santa outside, her eyebrows knit together with fury. She was fed up with his cruel wish fulfillment. He'd won. And now he must let her get on with her life. "I need to take back the wish! I've had enough, you hear me? Take it back."

Ro retreated to her room and sat on her bed, pondering her next move.

"Hey, what are you doing up here?" asked Gabby, startling her sister.

"What do you care?"

"Mom and Dad are worried about you. Don't you care about their feelings?"

"Nobody asked me about my feelings," said Ro, hugging her favorite penguin stuffed animal.

"Well, you're not the only one going through a rough time right now, you know. I miss the way things were as much as you do. But you're younger than me. You don't remember what it was like. You don't have to remember all the fighting. Everyone is happier now. Families change."

Ro choked up but refused to let her sister see her cry. Instead, she flicked away a tear. "I'm not happier. I don't want our family to change."

"I know. And I didn't, either. But it already did—the day you were born. Everything changed. You were new, and I definitely didn't like it. But then I saw how happy you made Mom and Dad. So I decided to give you a chance. Even though you annoy the heck out of me most of the time, you'll always be my little sister. I wouldn't change that for anything. Everything is going to be okay. I promise."

Ro let go. She cried into her sister's shoulder as Gabby pulled her in for a hug. At least Gabby understood; for that Ro was grateful. And when she thought about it, Ro realized she wouldn't change the fact that Gabby was her sister for anything, either. "I'm sorry I took your laptop. And your sketchbook. You're a really good artist."

Gabby waved her off. "You don't have to say that. But thanks. Come on, let's go downstairs."

"Hey, Gabby, I think I'll give new people a chance, too. But only because I've tried everything else. "

CHAPTER 17

Ro awoke the next morning like a whole new person. She was determined to spread some Christmas joy of her own. She started by bringing a mariachi band to the backyard to interrupt the family's game of What's That? Everyone rushed outside to enjoy the music, while her grandparents danced together happily in the window.

The next Christmas Day, when Louie played ghost, Ro went with it and screamed. Louie giggled in delight as he revealed himself.

"Did you know it was me?" He looked up at Ro hopefully.

For once, Ro decided not to break his heart. "I was totally surprised."

Satisfied, Louie asked, "Do you wanna be the ghost?"

"Not really," Ro said, shrugging.

The silly grin faded from Louie's face. He turned away from Ro and looked at the floor.

"Hey, Louie?" Hearing Ro's voice, Louie spun back around and came face to face with . . . a sheet ghost! "Boo!" He screamed with scared delight and was still cracking up when Ro revealed herself beneath the sheet.

"That was so good," squealed Louie.

Ro was surprised by how good it felt to make Louie happy.

"Let's go downstairs!" said Louie. "It's Christmas!"

"Hang on, your shoelace is untied." Ro crouched down and, for the second time that morning, treated Louie with kindness.

This Christmas, Louie and Ro ran down the stairs together. Louie leapt.

"Gotcha, you little devil," exclaimed Mike, catching him in his arms.

"Incoming!" yelped Ro, jumping from the stairs onto Mike's back. It dawned on Ro that Mike had enough room to hold both of them.

"What is this, a wrestling match?" asked Mike. He lifted both kids, one over each shoulder, fireman-style, and walked into the kitchen. "All right, which one of you is the Rock, and which one is John Cena? Guess who decided to join us."

"Morning, sleepy head," said Carolina.

Diane's face lit up when she saw the three of them together. "Rowena! Merry Christmas! Your dad told me that you made the softball team. That is amazing. What position do you play?"

This time, Rowena dispensed with her sarcasm. "Um, shortstop. But coach wants me to practice pitching."

Diane's eyes grew extra wide with what seemed to Ro to be genuine interest. "That's incredible, sweetie! Well, you're especially going to love your present today."

Mike glanced at his girlfriend. "Diane, don't ruin it."

Diane ignored Mike's plea and whispered into Ro's ear. "Let's just say it's really going to help you out on the team."

Mike chuckled. "Sorry, sprout. She's just excited 'cause she picked it out herself."

"Diane picked out the glove?" She'd thought that

Diane took no real interest in her, that Diane and Louie were just there to try to replace her and Gabby. Maybe she'd underestimated Diane. Maybe she wasn't so bad. "Cool."

When Abuelo Hector and Abuela Sofia arrived, Ro made sure that things went differently this Christmas.

"Oh, my little Rowena! Did you like your sweater? I made it myself," said Sofia, cupping Ro's face in her hands.

"We haven't opened presents yet, Mom," said Carolina.

"But I bet I'm going to love it, Abuela. And look what I made you. It's an herbal tea I found in the kitchen. It's supposed to be great for your upset tummy."

"Gracias, mi cariño!"

Christmas was already reindeer leaps ahead of the last version. Ro led Louie outside to play catch. As they tossed the ball around, they heard Gretchen arguing with two kids across the street. Ro and Louie crossed to get a better look.

"But that money is for charity," explained the boy, jumping in vain to reach for the container Gretchen had taken.

Gretchen growled. "Maybe I've got a charity of my own. It's called 'get over it'!"

Old Ro would have retreated across the street, back to her own problems. But new Ro decided to do something about the unfortunate situation. "Give them their money, Gretchen."

"And what are you gonna do about it?"

Ro lunged for the plastic container filled with cash, but Gretchen tripped her, laughing as Ro tumbled into an inflatable lawn gingerbread man. Ro just grinned, already plotting how she'd come better prepared next Christmas.

The next day, she tried to bring out Gretchen's kind side by giving her a Christmas present. Unfortunately, she ended up getting thrown into the gingerbread man again.

Ro and Louie learned judo from Uncle Bruce on the next couple of Christmases. Dressed in their new judogis, she and Louie were eager students. He even tried to motivate them with lofty quotes like, "It is not important to be better than someone else but to be better than yesterday."

While Louie reset as a beginner each Christmas, Ro grew in skill and confidence each day, determined to be better than the day before. And not just at judo.

On Christmas fifty-one, Ro was ready to put her finely tuned judo skills to the test.

"That's enough, Gretchen. I'm warning you. Give it back."

Gretchen was not one to take a challenge lightly. "And what are you gonna do about it?"

Ro reached for the container, a move that baited Gretchen into shifting her weight. Ro took advantage, executing an impressive lifting-hip throw that propelled Gretchen back several feet, right into the inflatable gingerbread man. Everyone erupted in cheers; Ro had saved the day. And she realized it felt incredible to do so.

"I believe this is yours," she said, returning the money. Her new friends, who introduced themselves as Holly and Wyatt, were grateful.

"Thank you," Holly said, smiling. "And I believe this is yours. On the house. Wyatt, take it away."

Wyatt stepped forward and projected his voice,

as if playing to a full house. "What did one plate say to another plate?"

"I give up," said Ro.

Wyatt jumped up and down, barely able to contain himself as he delivered the punch line. "Dinner is on me!"

Ro and Louie both cracked up at the joke.

"Is this your little brother?" asked Holly, nodding toward Louie.

Louie looked up at Ro expectantly as she considered the question. If her dad and Diane were getting married, then Louie would technically become her half brother. But doing anything halfway was no way to be a family. Ro was going all in. "Yup, that's right," she said. Louie smiled big.

Ro turned back toward Holly and Wyatt. "It's Christmas. Why the heck are you out here selling jokes?"

Holly clapped her mittened hand around her brother's shoulder. "It makes us feel good to help others. That's what Christmas is about."

"Daddy says everyone should do what they can and every little bit helps," said Wyatt.

As Ro continued to repeat her Christmas Day, she

found more ways to help those around her. Instead of watching Mrs. Brown cry over spilled eggs, Ro ran forward with her own reusable bag and caught the falling groceries in midair. She even helped her get her groceries home.

At Winterfest, number one on her list of favorite Christmas memories, Ro found Frankie on one knee proposing to Winston as a windblown ornament careered toward Frankie's head. Ro leapt behind the couple, catching the glass ornament seconds before it crashed.

"That would've totally hit her," said Winston.

Frankie stared at Ro, flabbergasted. "How'd you know that would happen?"

Ro looked at Frankie's hand, interwoven with Winston's. "Don't you have a better question, to ask him?"

"Right," chirped Frankie, turning to Winston. "Marry me?"

"Yes!" shouted Winston as he swept up his fiancée in his arms.

Ro decided to email Santa to update him on her latest Christmases.

Hey Santa, I just wanted to thank you for showing me the true meaning of family. Thanks for the lesson, Big Guy. Now I think I've got some people to go help.

Ro and Louie helped Wyatt and Holly upgrade their door-to-door joke-selling operation to a permanent joke stand on their driveway. Neighbors lined up, wanting to hear a joke and donate to a good cause. Even Gretchen.

Ro used her tuna trap for goodwill, too. She set down the can near the bushes, lured out Cupcake—and her kittens—then took them home to Shaun and Linda.

"Was that Rowena?" asked Linda as she opened the front door to find a beautifully wrapped gift box.

"Cupcake! My gosh, it's a miracle," sang Shaun, beaming at the cat, who pranced through the front door like she owned the place. Shaun took the lid off the present. Inside were the two most adorable kittens he'd ever seen. Linda and Shaun hugged each other. It was, indeed, a very happy Christmas.

CHAPTER 18

On Christmas Day fifty-six, Ro decided to spread cheer in her very own house. If she couldn't make family Christmas like it had been in the past, she might as well make it the best it could be in the present.

As Ro joined her family for presents, she walked around the room, picking up all the crumpled wrapping paper. Ro sensed her mom's joy and surprise. "Just being helpful. I wouldn't want anyone to break their neck."

"Aw, Ro," said Carolina. "This is better than any present I could think of."

Ro made a show of taking a big bite out of one of Diane's kale cookies and gave Diane a thumbs-up as she chewed. To Ro's shock, the vegetable-laden sweets weren't half bad.

"Carolina, your father and I wanted to give you something very special," Sofia began. Ro knew the next moments by heart: Abuela would talk about her bis-abuela, Gabby would accidentally fling Olive's slimy chew toy, and a catastrophic chain of events would follow. But this time, Ro was ready. She leapt up and snagged Olive's toy in midair. Her relatives continued to ooh and aah over the unscathed bowl.

Later that day, she came to Uncle Gerry's rescue. His nervousness was palpable as he got ready to deliver his stand-up routine. But this Christmas, Ro had his back. "You can do it, Uncle Gerry. You're the funniest person I know," she said, taking her uncle's hand in hers.

Gerry took a deep breath, smiled at Ro, and began his routine. The room cracked up; Gerry gained confidence. "What did I tell you? You killed it!" Uncle Bruce told him.

Gerry fist-bumped Ro in gratitude. "Thanks, Ro!"

There was a knock on the front door as the family settled in for the evening. Carolina looked puzzled; she wasn't expecting anyone. She opened the door to find

Mr. and Mrs. Brown from down the street all bundled up and holding a red-foil loaf pan.

"Merry Christmas, Carolina! I baked banana bread," said Mrs. Brown, handing her the treat.

"Oh my, you didn't have to do that."

Mr. Brown gave a hearty belly laugh. "We wouldn't have the ingredients if it wasn't for your little Rowena."

Mrs. Brown nodded in agreement. "Is she here? We want to say thanks."

Carolina invited the Browns to join them. She was pleased to hear Ro had been a help to them.

The doorbell rang again. This time, it was their neighbors Linda and Shaun.

"Hey, Carolina," said Shaun. "I made bread pudding. I know it's Ro's favorite."

"She brought our Cupcake home. And the best Christmas gift ever: two new little babies!" chirped Linda.

"You raised the most wonderful girl. Can we say hello?"

Carolina invited them in and placed the bread

pudding on the dining room table next to the banana bread. When had Rowena found the time to return a lost cat? Carolina was in the kitchen when the doorbell rang again. It was Frankie and her fiancé, Winston.

"Merry Christmas!" shouted the happy couple.

Carolina looked dumbstruck. "Let me guess . . . Ro?"

Frankie held out her phone to share a picture. The image showed Frankie on one knee proposing to Winston in front of a heavily decorated tree. Ro stood between them, showing off a just-caught ornament and smiling.

"If we have a girl, we're naming her Rowena," Winston said.

"Let's not put the cart before the horse," said Frankie. As they stepped across the threshold and joined the others in the family room, there was another *tappity-tap-tap* on the door. By that point, Carolina was unfazed.

Wyatt, Holly, and their dad, Henry, stood at the doorway.

"Hi, oh, you're having a party. Sorry to interrupt," said Henry.

"You're not at all. How can I help?" Carolina's warm smile welcomed the trio.

"I'm Henry. These are my kids," he said. He had a friendly manner about him.

Ro ran up and pulled the kids into the house. "Mom, these are my new friends Holly and Wyatt. C'mon, you guys. I wanna show you my uncles' new dog!"

The kids scampered after Ro as Henry explained, "Ro helped them raise money for the foundation today."

Carolina raised an eyebrow. "I'm sorry, foundation?"

"It's just a small charity. The kids lost their mom a while back."

"I'm so sorry to hear that."

Henry nodded. "Anyways, we just moved to the neighborhood."

"Welcome," Carolina said.

"I think it's so nice they've already made friends."

Henry and Carolina lingered in the doorway a minute longer, until Abuela Sofia interrupted. "Bienvenidos! Carolina, why are you keeping our handsome guest in the doorway?" she said with a wink.

Carolina laughed and invited Henry inside for what was now a full-blown Christmas party. More neighbors and friends arrived, including Gretchen. Holly, Wyatt, and Uncle Gerry practiced jokes on one another. Abuela Sofia and Carolina, both wearing beautiful hand-embroidered aprons, tied a matching one around Diane. Ro circled the room, serving dessert. "Try my stepmom's kale cookies! It sounds weird, I know, but it's surprisingly delicious! And the green makes it super Christmassy!"

Later, Wyatt, Holly, Gretchen, and Louie were seated in a circle around Gabby, who was drawing for them in her sketchbook.

Ro motioned to Gabby. Gabby handed her markers to the kids and made her way to Ro.

She handed Gabby a holiday gift bag. "This one doesn't come with knobs."

Gabby unwrapped a new tablet. She was flabber-gasted.

"I used my savings," she told her sister.

"But I didn't get you anything."

But Gabby had. "You were there for me when I

needed you. I couldn't ask for more. Or a better big sister." Ro hugged Gabby hard. "Merry Christmas, Gabby."

A short while later, Ro gathered the guests in the family room. She looked out and felt a tingling satisfaction to see so many friends and relatives gathered together. "I'm so glad you all ended up here tonight. I did a lot today, you guys. I mean a lot a lot. But one thing I haven't done is thank my family."

Carolina put her hand to her mouth. "Aw, Ro. This is so unlike you."

"I know. It's sappy. But it's also Christmas. And none of you will remember this anyway."

Uncle Bruce held up his phone. "That's why we have cameras, honey."

Ro pushed up the sleeves of her sweater and continued. "So a long time ago someone wise told me Christmas isn't only about tradition. It's about spending time with the people you care about."

"I said that yesterday," said Carolina.

"I was getting to that, Mom. Quit hogging the limelight."

Everyone laughed at the exchange. "And you were

right. Because here we all are. Together. And I've never been happier. I've seen a lot of Christmases in my time. I mean a lot a lot. But this one definitely tops the list."

Mike and Carolina beamed. Abuela and Carolina began to sing a carol, and Ro joined in. Soon the whole room was singing in unison. It was a new Christmas tradition Ro would cherish for years to come.

Once the guests had gone home, the plates had been washed, and the music had been turned off, Carolina tucked Ro in. She noticed Ro's copy of *A Christmas Carol* on the bed.

"Are you reading this?" she asked, sounding impressed.

"I finished it this morning," said Ro.

"And? What did you think?"

"I get why it's a classic. Some parts were a little scary. But he needed to go through it."

"And why's that?"

"So he could become a better person. Someone who's not afraid of letting new people in. It's never too late for a reset."

Carolina snuggled with her daughter, looking

amazed. "How did I get the smartest girl?" She kissed Ro good night.

"Hey, Mom? I had a great Christmas. Even if you don't remember any of this tomorrow, I'm happy." It was true. After so many Christmases, Rowena finally had one that would land at the very top of her top five list.

"Honey, what are you talking about? Of course I'll remember."

"But just in case you don't, I'm still glad we had today."

"I'm happy, too, Rowena. Merry Christmas."

Ro went to sleep, ready to wake up and face yet another Christmas Day.

CHAPTER 19

The next morning, Ro awoke to the familiar sound of "Jingle Bells." But this time, Louie was sans ghost costume.

"Wake up! Wake up!" he said, shaking Ro's arm.

On the radio, the DJ cut in. "We can finally retire that song until next year."

Ro sat up, unsure if she should believe what she had just heard. "Louie? Where's your white sheet?" she asked.

"You wanna play ghost?"

"No! Is it still Christmas?"

Louie shook his head. "Christmas was yesterday."

Ro's eyes widened. "It's over!" she shouted. "Christmas is finally over!"

Ro bolted down the stairs, but Mike wasn't waiting at the bottom to catch her. She ran into the kitchen. It was empty. Everything was different from the day before. She and Louie finally found Carolina and Gabby shivering on the driveway in their pajamas, watching Mike and Diane load their car.

Mike closed the trunk and smiled at Ro. "There you are, sprout. We were about to find you to say goodbye."

"You're leaving already?" she asked.

"Why? You haven't had enough of us?" Mike asked.

"I'm really glad you came, Diane." Ro surprised everyone by throwing her arms around Diane's waist and pulling her in for a real hug.

Diane was touched. "It was good to see you, Ro. I can't wait to do this again next year."

Ro jumped in. "What are you guys doing for New Year's? Or President's Day? Don't you have a birthday coming up, Dad?"

Mike and Diane traded smiles, clearly thrilled by Ro's acceptance of their new family. Mike hugged Ro, then slid right into their elaborate handshake. "I love you, sprout. See you soon."

"Later, Louie," said Ro. Then she and Louie performed her and Mike's elaborate handshake.

"Nice," said Mike. "We'd better get going. Bye, you guys!"

As their car pulled out, it passed a white limo parked on the street. Inside sat Tall Santa.

"Who wants breakfast?" asked Carolina, heading inside with Gabby. "Chocolate chip pancakes?"

"I'll be right there," yelled Ro, already jogging out to the limo. She gave Tall Santa the side-eye. "Where the heck have you been?"

Santa stroked his goatee. "Gimme a break, kid. It has been a really, really long day."

"Tell me about it," said Ro.

"So? Did you get through your list?"

Ro shrugged. "Hey, how did you know about my list?"

"I've been known to keep a few of my own. Nothing fancy like yours," said Santa, nodding to a big scroll that lay open in the passenger seat. On it were inscribed the names of thousands of kids.

Ro was skeptical. "What is that supposed to be? The naughty list?"

"I think of it more like a second-chance list. Deep down even the naughtiest kids want to be nice. Some just need a little more time."

Ro had to know. "Okay, so how did I do?"

Tall Santa checked the naughty list—twice—and found Rowena Clybourne on it. But then her name disappeared before her very eyes. Magic.

"Ro," called Carolina from the porch.

"I'd better go. Thanks, Santa!" Rowena said.

Santa exchanged knowing smiles with Ro.

Rowena headed for her front door but turned for a final look. Tall Santa's limo floated upward, then flew across the sky.

It had been the best Christmas (well, Christmases) of Rowena's life.